BLACK PANTHER

A NATION UNDER OUR FEET: PART 2

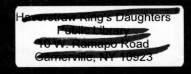

Spotlight

ABDOBOOKS.COM

Reinforced library bound edition published in 2020 by Spotlight,
a division of ABDO, PO Box 398166, Minneapolis, Minnesota 55439.
Spotlight produces high-quality reinforced library bound editions for
schools and libraries. Published by agreement with Marvel Characters, Inc.

Printed in the United States of America, North Mankato, Minnesota.
042019
092019

THIS BOOK CONTAINS
RECYCLED MATERIALS

© 2020 MARVEL

Library of Congress Control Number: 2018965952

Publisher's Cataloging-in-Publication Data

Names: Coates, Ta-Nehisi, author. | Stelfreeze, Brian; Martin, Laura; Sprouse, Chris;
    Story, Karl, illustrators.
Title: A nation under our feet / writer: Ta-Nehisi Coates; art: Brian Stelfreeze ; Laura
    Martin ; Chris Sprouse ; Karl Story.
Description: Minneapolis, Minnesota : Spotlight, 2020 | Series: Black Panther
Summary: With a dramatic upheaval in Wakanda on the horizon, T'Challa knows his
    kingdom needs to change to survive, but he struggles to find balance in his
    roles as king and the Black Panther.
Identifiers: ISBN 9781532143519 (pt. 1 ; lib. bdg.) | ISBN 9781532143526 (pt. 2 ; lib.
    bdg.) | ISBN 9781532143533 (pt. 3 ; lib. bdg.) | ISBN 9781532143540 (pt. 4 ;
    lib. bdg.) | ISBN 9781532143557 (pt. 5 ; lib. bdg.) | ISBN 9781532143564 (pt.
    6 ; lib. bdg.)
Subjects: LCSH: Black Panther (Fictitious character)--Juvenile fiction. | Superheroes--
    Juvenile fiction. | Kings and rulers--Juvenile fiction. | Graphic novels--Juvenile
    fiction. | T'Challa, of Wakanda (Fictitious character)--Juvenile fiction.
Classification: DDC 741.5--dc23

Spotlight

A Division of ABDO
abdobooks.com

BLACK PANTHER

T'CHALLA, KING OF WAKANDA AND KNOWN THE WORLD OVER AS **BLACK PANTHER**, ATTEMPTED TO PACIFY A MINERS' STRIKE WHEN A MYSTERIOUS WOMAN NAMED **ZENZI** TURNED IT INTO A FULL-BLOWN RIOT BY SOMEHOW UNLEASHING THE RAGE WITHIN BOTH THE MINERS AND T'CHALLA'S SOLDIERS.

ELSEWHERE, **ANEKA** -- FORMERLY CAPTAIN OF T'CHALLA'S ROYAL GUARD, THE **DORA MILAJE** -- WAS SENTENCED TO DEATH FOR KILLING A CORRUPT WAKANDAN CHIEFTAIN. HER LOVER AND FELLOW DORA MILAJE, **AYO**, USED STOLEN **MIDNIGHT ANGEL** ARMOR TO FREE ANEKA, AND TOGETHER THEY FLED THE GOLDEN CITY.

MEANWHILE, T'CHALLA AGONIZES OVER HIS SISTER **SHURI'S** CURRENT STATE OF BEING TRAPPED BETWEEN LIFE AND DEATH, DESPITE HIS CONTINUED EFFORTS TO REVERSE THIS.

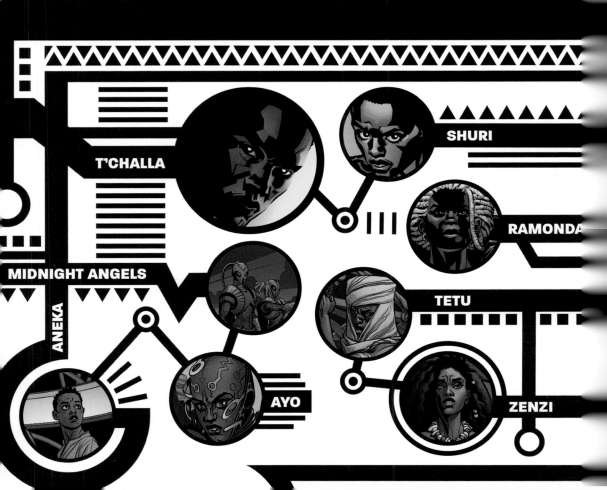

T'CHALLA

SHURI

RAMONDA

MIDNIGHT ANGELS

ANEKA

TETU

AYO

ZENZI

A NATION
UNDER OUR FEET
part 2

writer **TA-NEHISI COATES**
artist **BRIAN STELFREEZE**
color artist **LAURA MARTIN**

letterer **VC's JOE SABINO**
design **MANNY MEDEROS**
logo **RIAN HUGHES**
cover by **BRIAN STELFREEZE**
and **LAURA MARTIN**
variant covers by
FRANK CHO
SANFORD GREENE
JAMAL CAMPBELL

assistant editor **CHRIS ROBINSON**
editor **WIL MOSS**
executive editor **TOM BREVOORT**

editor in chief **AXEL ALONSO** chief creative officer **JOE QUESADA**
publisher **DAN BUCKLEY** executive producer **ALAN FINE**

BLACK PANTHER

created by
STAN LEE &
JACK KIRBY

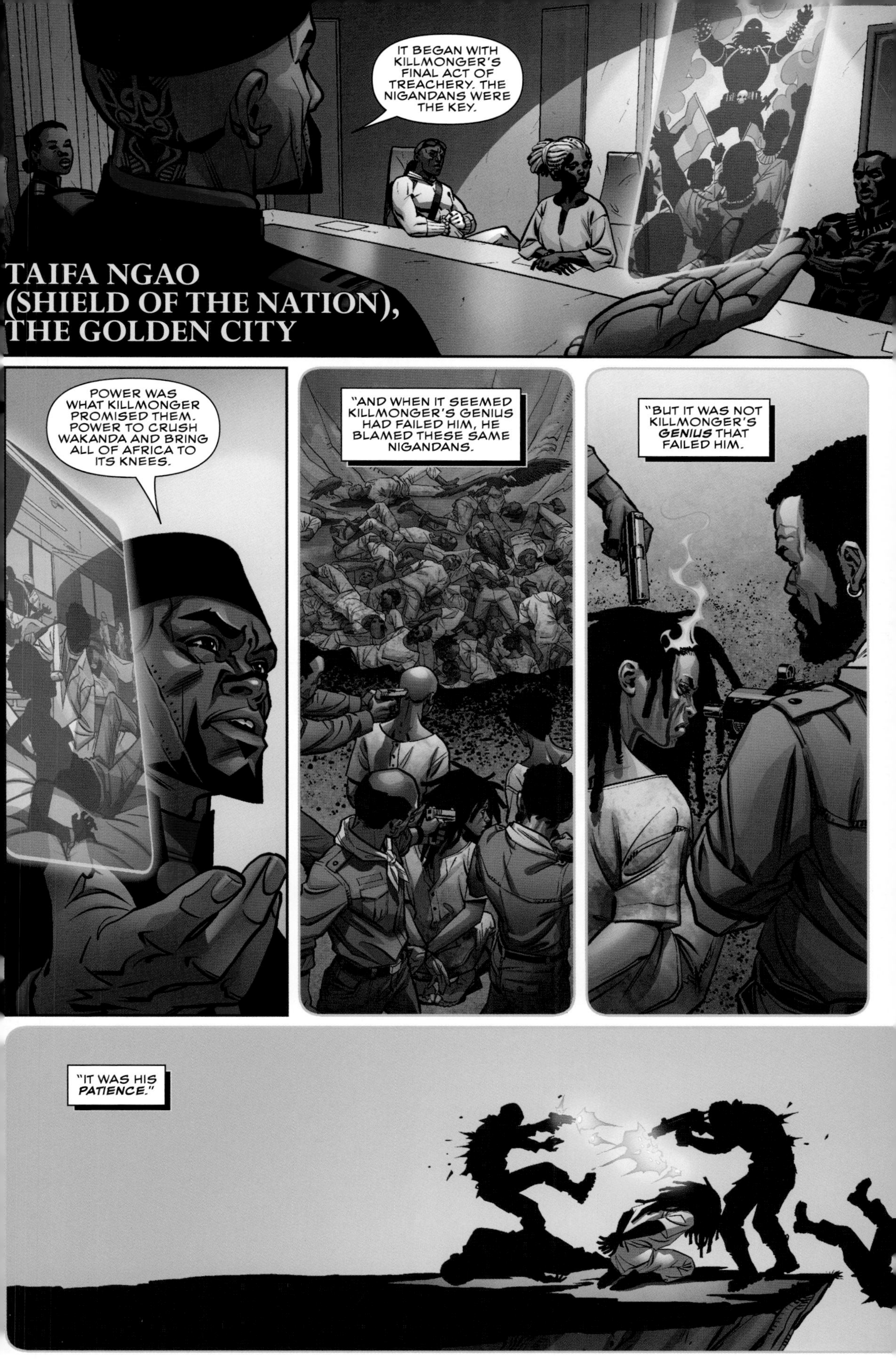
IT BEGAN WITH KILLMONGER'S FINAL ACT OF TREACHERY. THE NIGANDANS WERE THE KEY.
TAIFA NGAO (SHIELD OF THE NATION), THE GOLDEN CITY
POWER WAS WHAT KILLMONGER PROMISED THEM. POWER TO CRUSH WAKANDA AND BRING ALL OF AFRICA TO ITS KNEES.
"AND WHEN IT SEEMED KILLMONGER'S GENIUS HAD FAILED HIM, HE BLAMED THESE SAME NIGANDANS.
"BUT IT WAS NOT KILLMONGER'S *GENIUS* THAT FAILED HIM.
"IT WAS HIS *PATIENCE*."

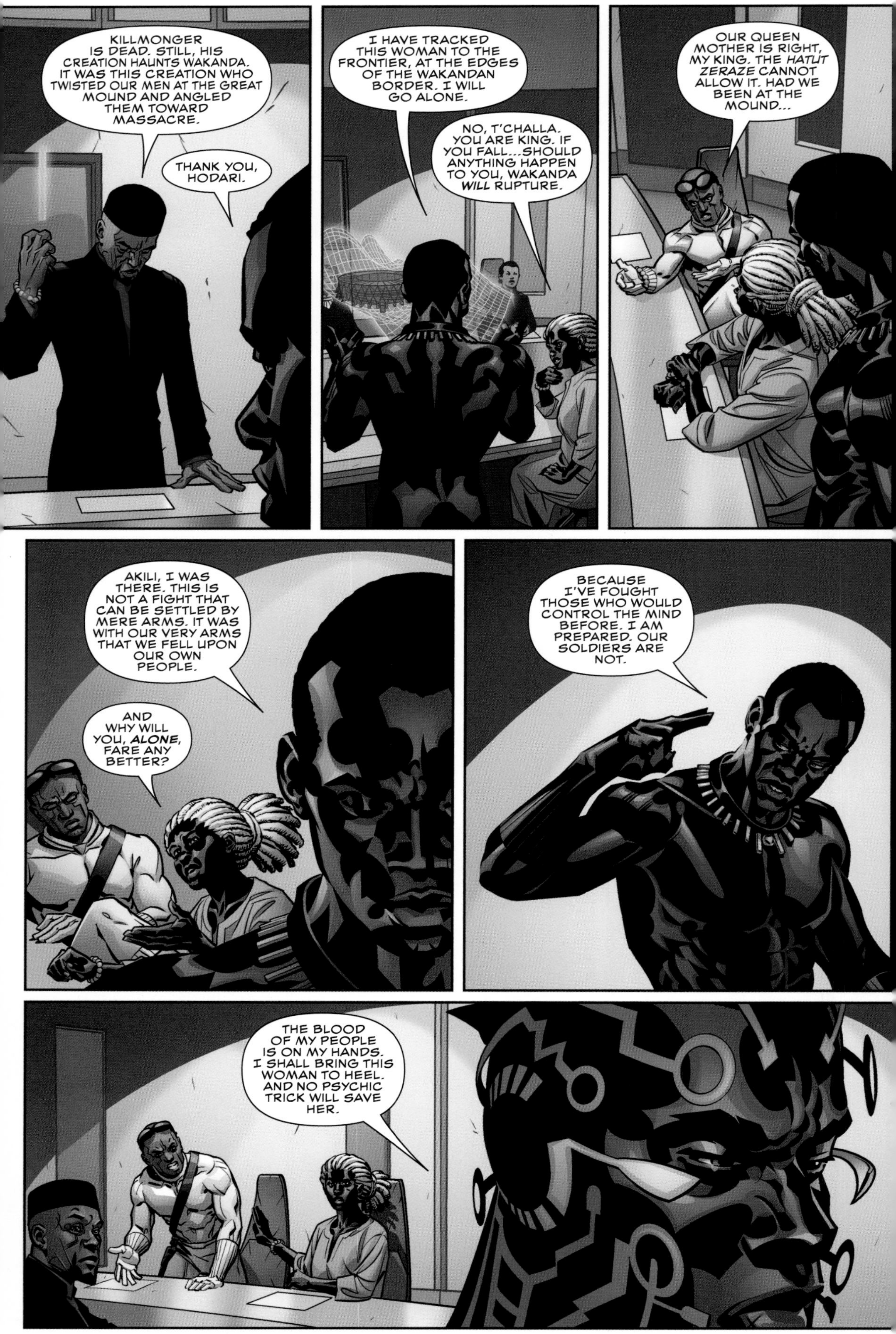
KILLMONGER IS DEAD. STILL, HIS CREATION HAUNTS WAKANDA. IT WAS THIS CREATION WHO TWISTED OUR MEN AT THE GREAT MOUND AND ANGLED THEM TOWARD MASSACRE.
THANK YOU, HODARI.
I HAVE TRACKED THIS WOMAN TO THE FRONTIER, AT THE EDGES OF THE WAKANDAN BORDER. I WILL GO ALONE.
NO, T'CHALLA. YOU ARE KING. IF YOU FALL...SHOULD ANYTHING HAPPEN TO YOU, WAKANDA *WILL* RUPTURE.
OUR QUEEN MOTHER IS RIGHT, MY KING. THE *HATUT ZERAZE* CANNOT ALLOW IT. HAD WE BEEN AT THE MOUND...
AKILI, I WAS THERE. THIS IS NOT A FIGHT THAT CAN BE SETTLED BY MERE ARMS. IT WAS WITH OUR VERY ARMS THAT WE FELL UPON OUR OWN PEOPLE.
AND WHY WILL YOU, *ALONE*, FARE ANY BETTER?
BECAUSE I'VE FOUGHT THOSE WHO WOULD CONTROL THE MIND BEFORE. I AM PREPARED. OUR SOLDIERS ARE NOT.
THE BLOOD OF MY PEOPLE IS ON MY HANDS. I SHALL BRING THIS WOMAN TO HEEL. AND NO PSYCHIC TRICK WILL SAVE HER.

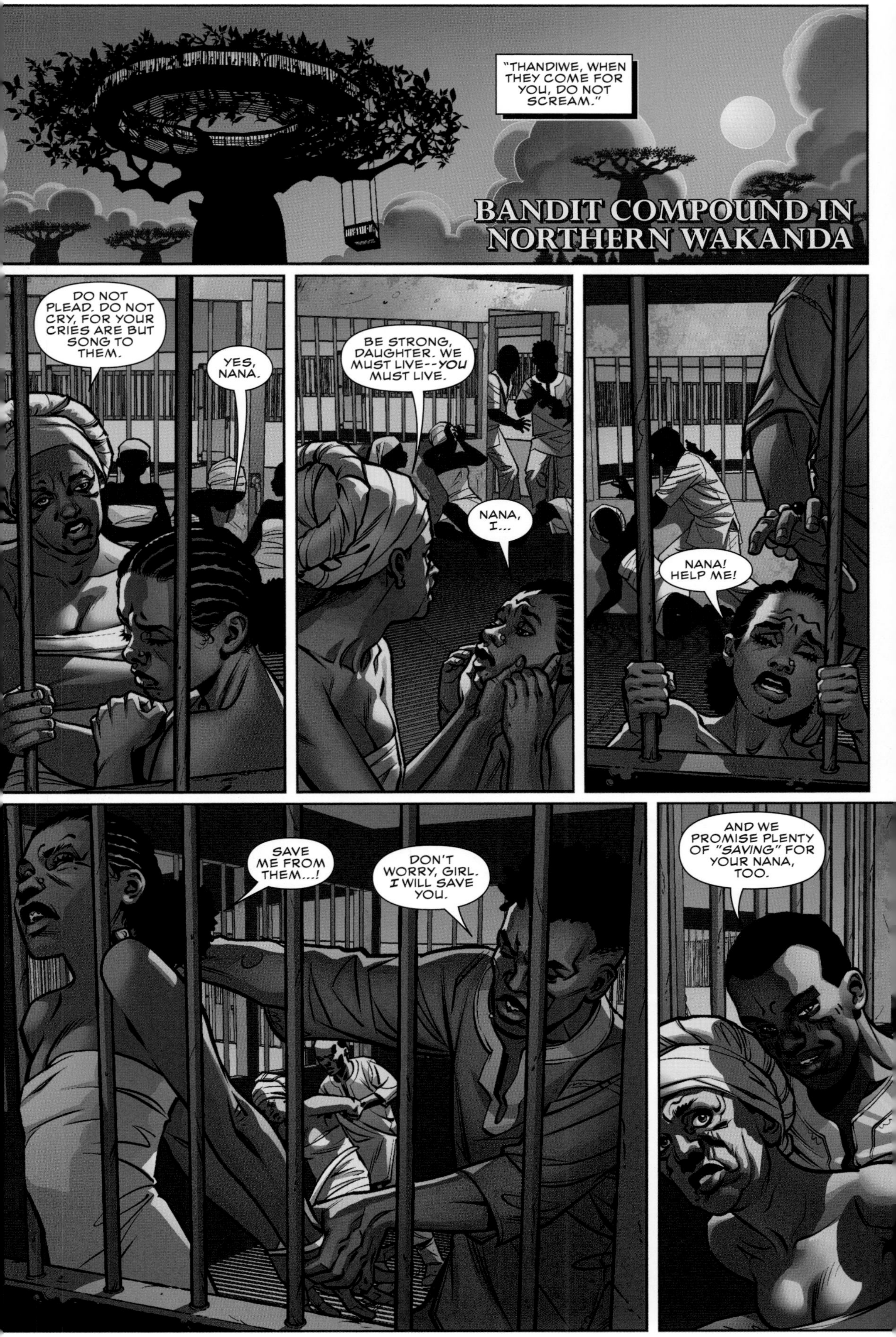
"THANDIWE, WHEN THEY COME FOR YOU, DO NOT SCREAM."
BANDIT COMPOUND IN NORTHERN WAKANDA
DO NOT PLEAD. DO NOT CRY, FOR YOUR CRIES ARE BUT SONG TO THEM.
YES, NANA.
BE STRONG, DAUGHTER. WE MUST LIVE--YOU MUST LIVE.
NANA, I...
NANA! HELP ME!
SAVE ME FROM THEM...!
DON'T WORRY, GIRL. I WILL SAVE YOU.
AND WE PROMISE PLENTY OF "SAVING" FOR YOUR NANA, TOO.

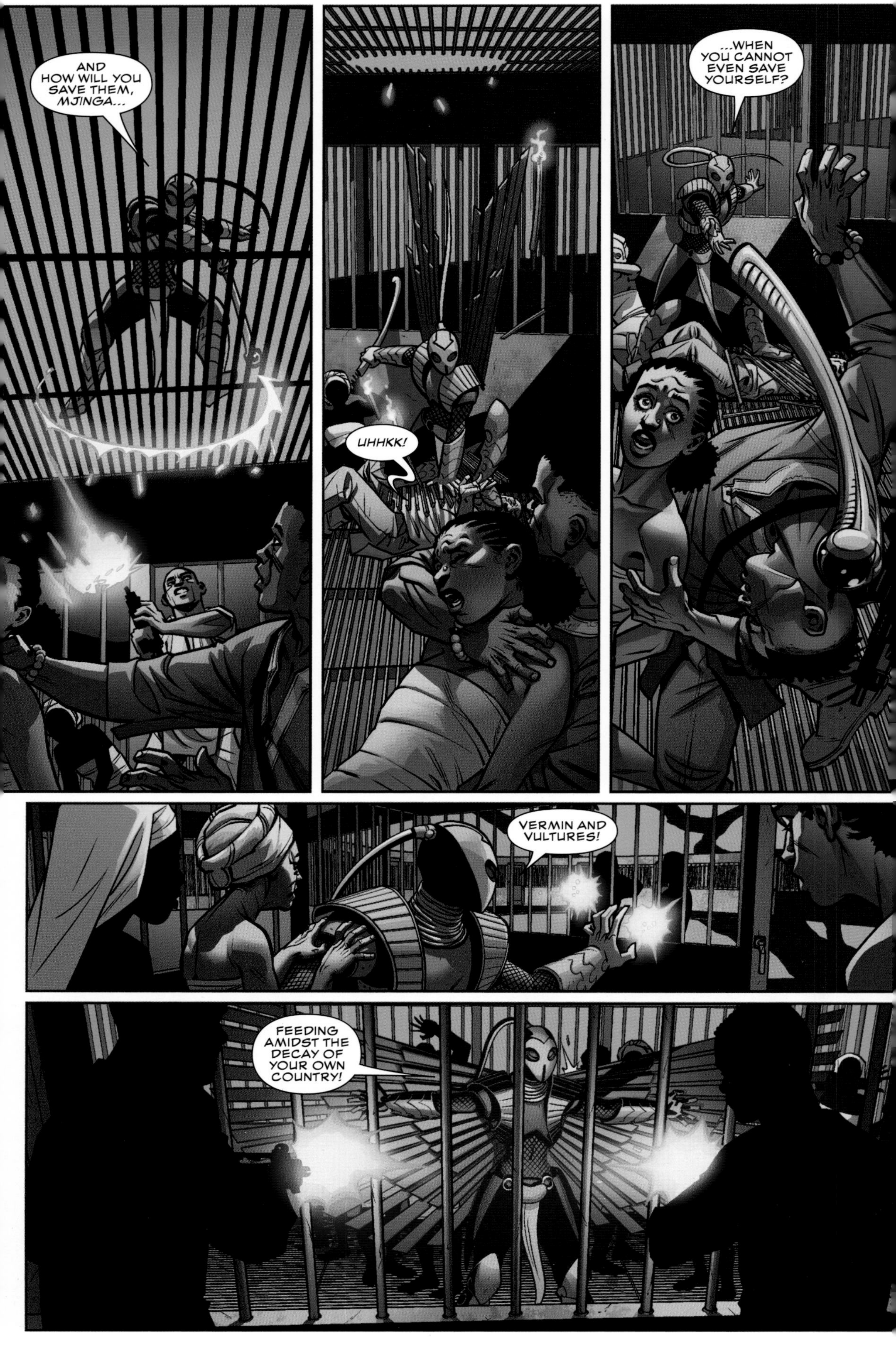
AND HOW WILL YOU SAVE THEM, MJINGA...
UHHKK!
...WHEN YOU CANNOT EVEN SAVE YOURSELF?
VERMIN AND VULTURES!
FEEDING AMIDST THE DECAY OF YOUR OWN COUNTRY!

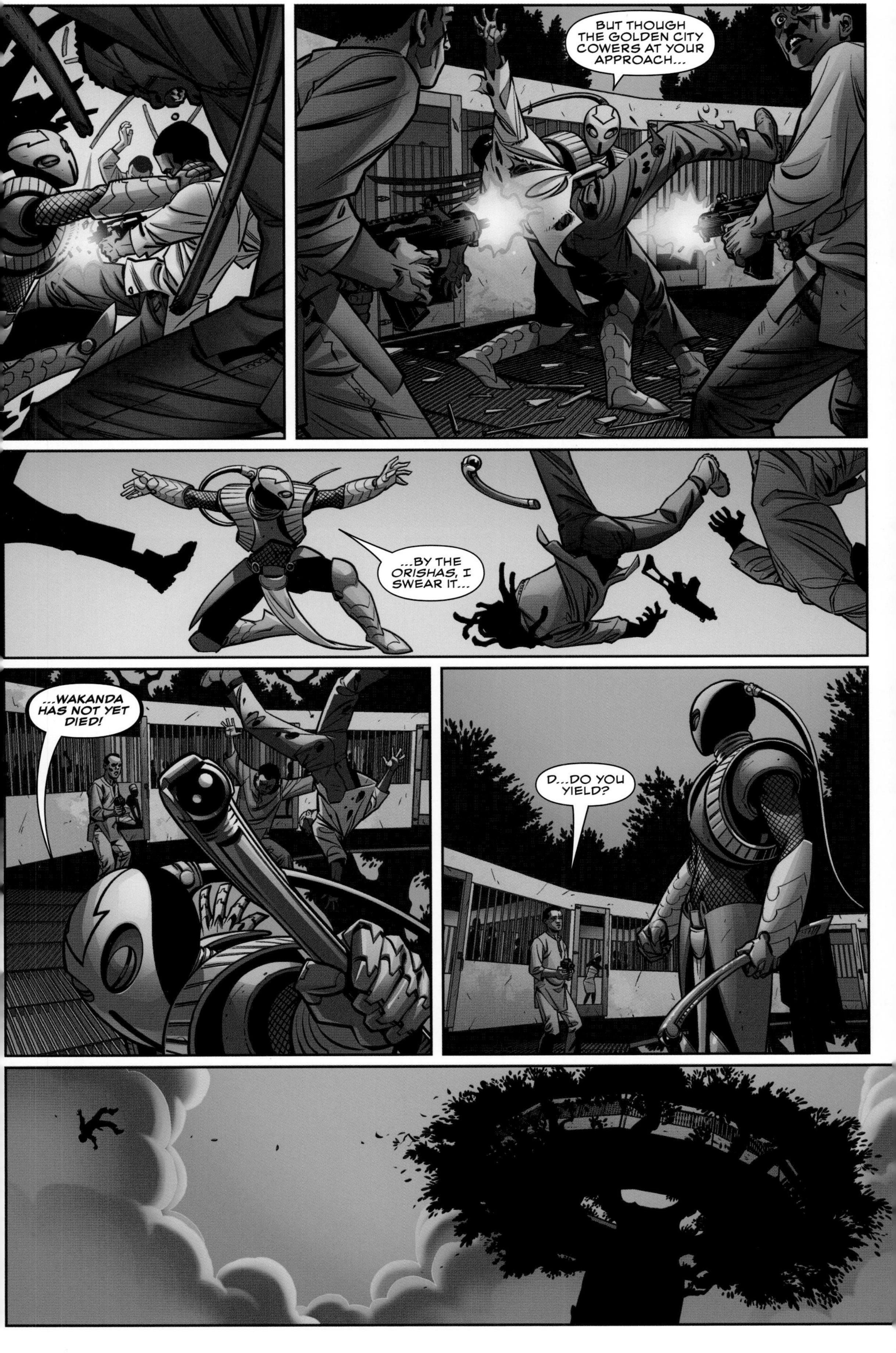
BUT THOUGH THE GOLDEN CITY COWERS AT YOUR APPROACH...
...BY THE ORISHAS, I SWEAR IT...
...WAKANDA HAS NOT YET DIED!
D...DO YOU YIELD?

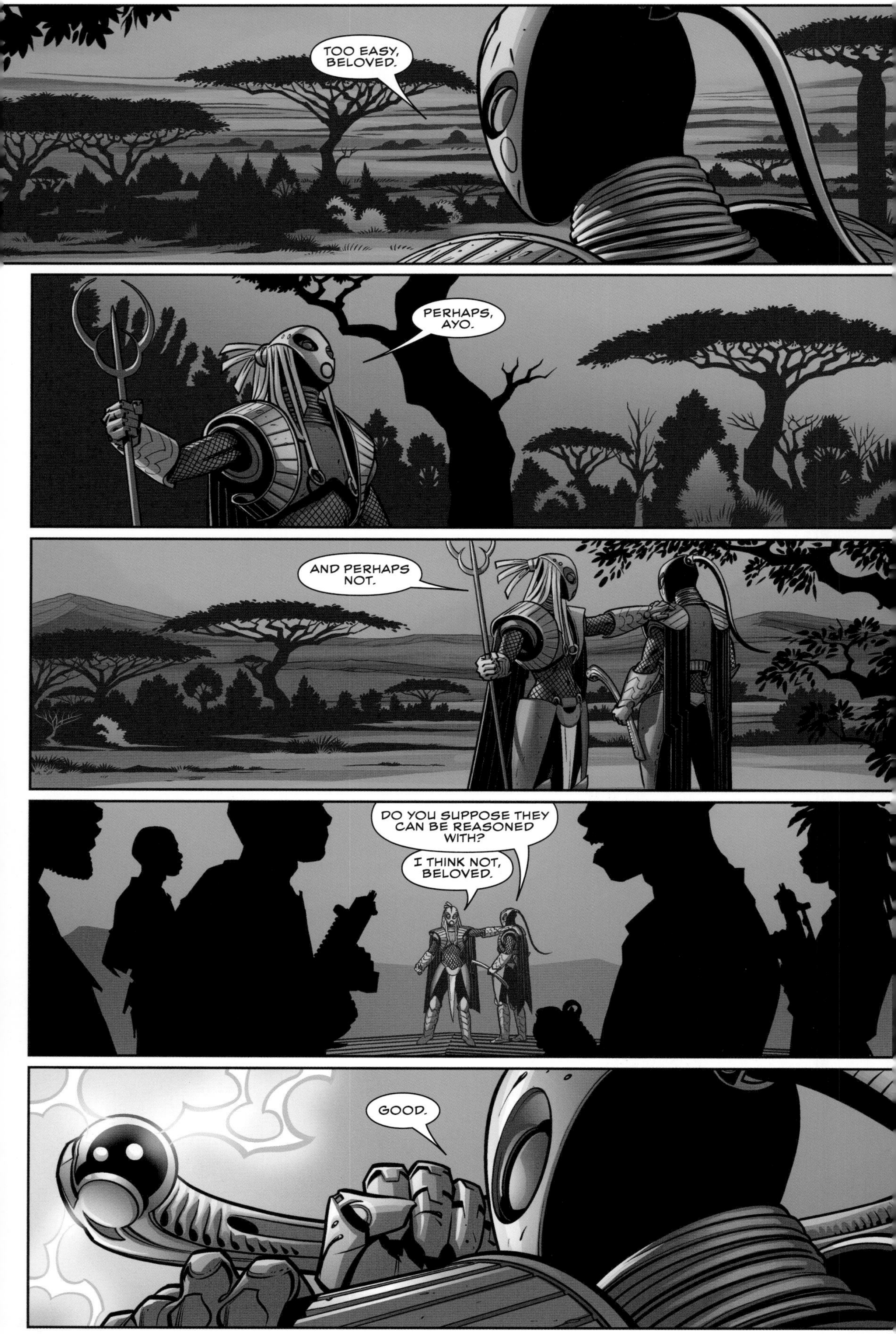
TOO EASY, BELOVED.
PERHAPS, AYO.
AND PERHAPS NOT.
DO YOU SUPPOSE THEY CAN BE REASONED WITH?
I THINK NOT, BELOVED.
GOOD.

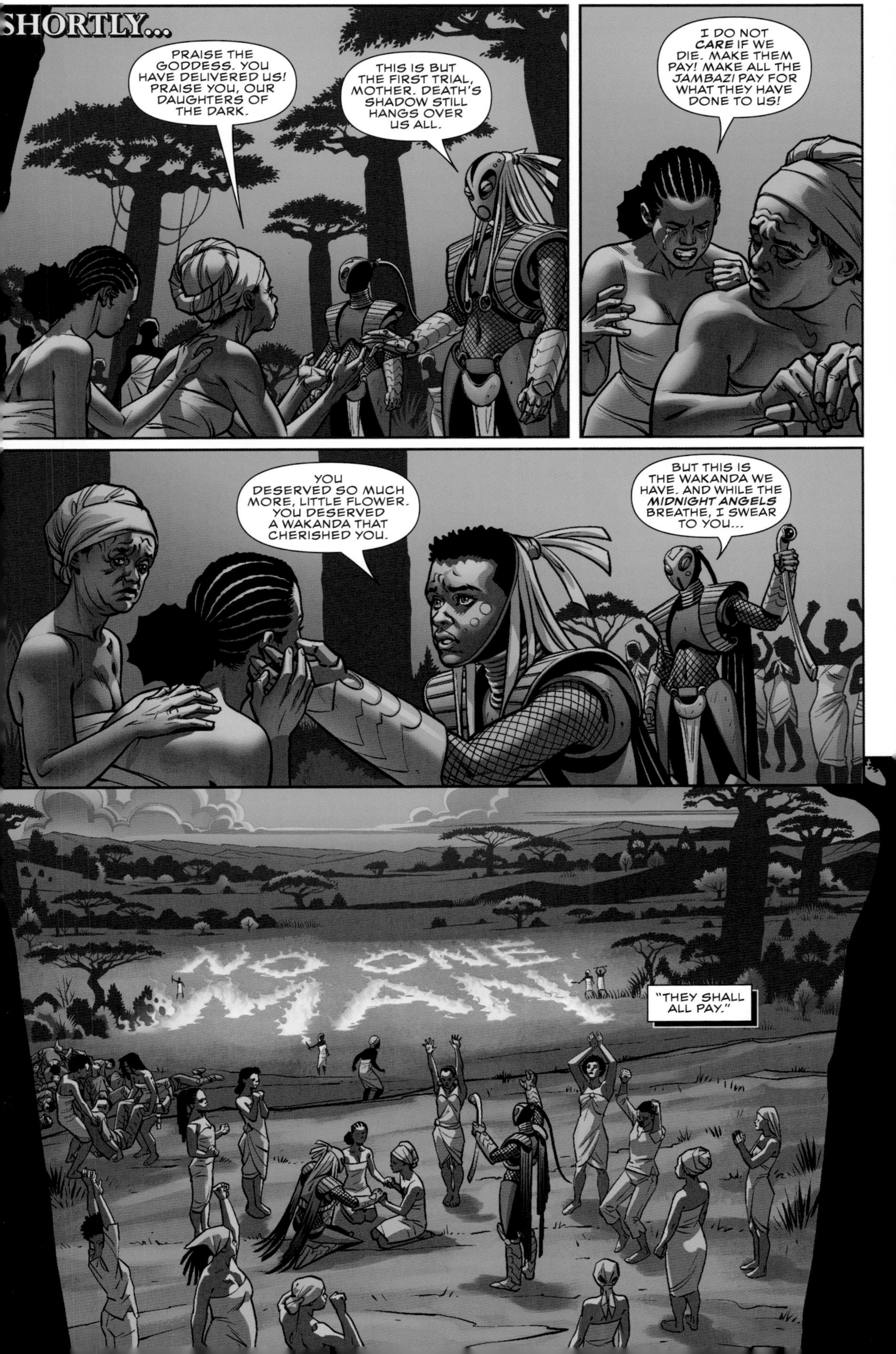
SHORTLY...
PRAISE THE GODDESS. YOU HAVE DELIVERED US! PRAISE YOU, OUR DAUGHTERS OF THE DARK.
THIS IS BUT THE FIRST TRIAL, MOTHER. DEATH'S SHADOW STILL HANGS OVER US ALL.
I DO NOT *CARE* IF WE DIE. MAKE THEM PAY! MAKE ALL THE *JAMBAZI* PAY FOR WHAT THEY HAVE DONE TO US!
YOU DESERVED SO MUCH MORE, LITTLE FLOWER. YOU DESERVED A WAKANDA THAT CHERISHED YOU.
BUT THIS IS THE WAKANDA WE HAVE. AND WHILE THE *MIDNIGHT ANGELS* BREATHE, I SWEAR TO YOU...
"THEY SHALL ALL PAY."

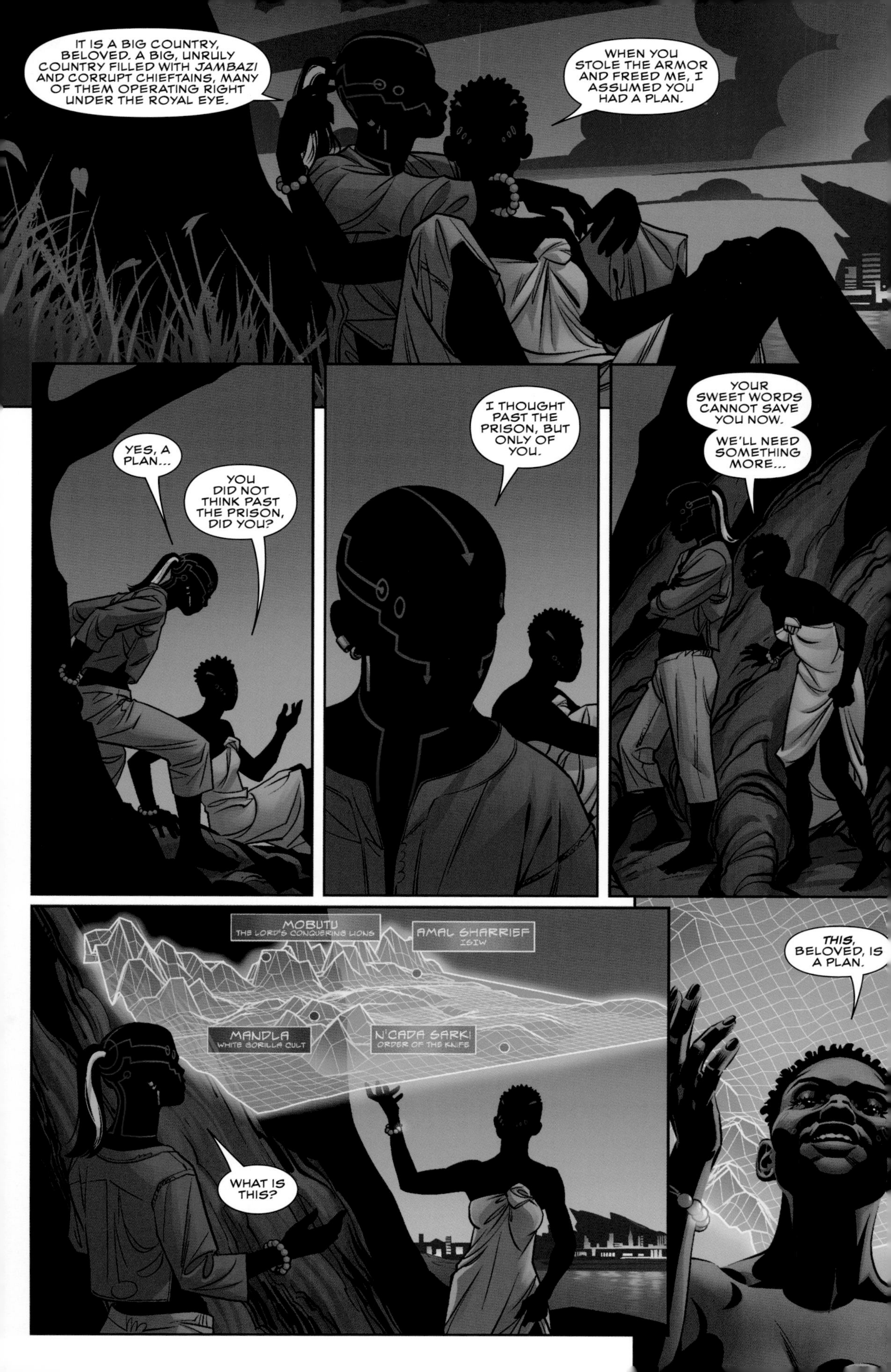
IT IS A BIG COUNTRY, BELOVED. A BIG, UNRULY COUNTRY FILLED WITH *JAMBAZI* AND CORRUPT CHIEFTAINS, MANY OF THEM OPERATING RIGHT UNDER THE ROYAL EYE.
WHEN YOU STOLE THE ARMOR AND FREED ME, I ASSUMED YOU HAD A PLAN.
YES, A PLAN...
YOU DID NOT THINK PAST THE PRISON, DID YOU?
I THOUGHT PAST THE PRISON, BUT ONLY OF YOU.
YOUR SWEET WORDS CANNOT SAVE YOU NOW.
WE'LL NEED SOMETHING MORE...
MOBUTU
THE LORD'S CONQUERING LIONS
AMAL SHARRIEF
ISIW
MANDLA
WHITE GORILLA CULT
N'CADA SARKI
ORDER OF THE KNIFE
WHAT IS THIS?
THIS, BELOVED, IS A PLAN.

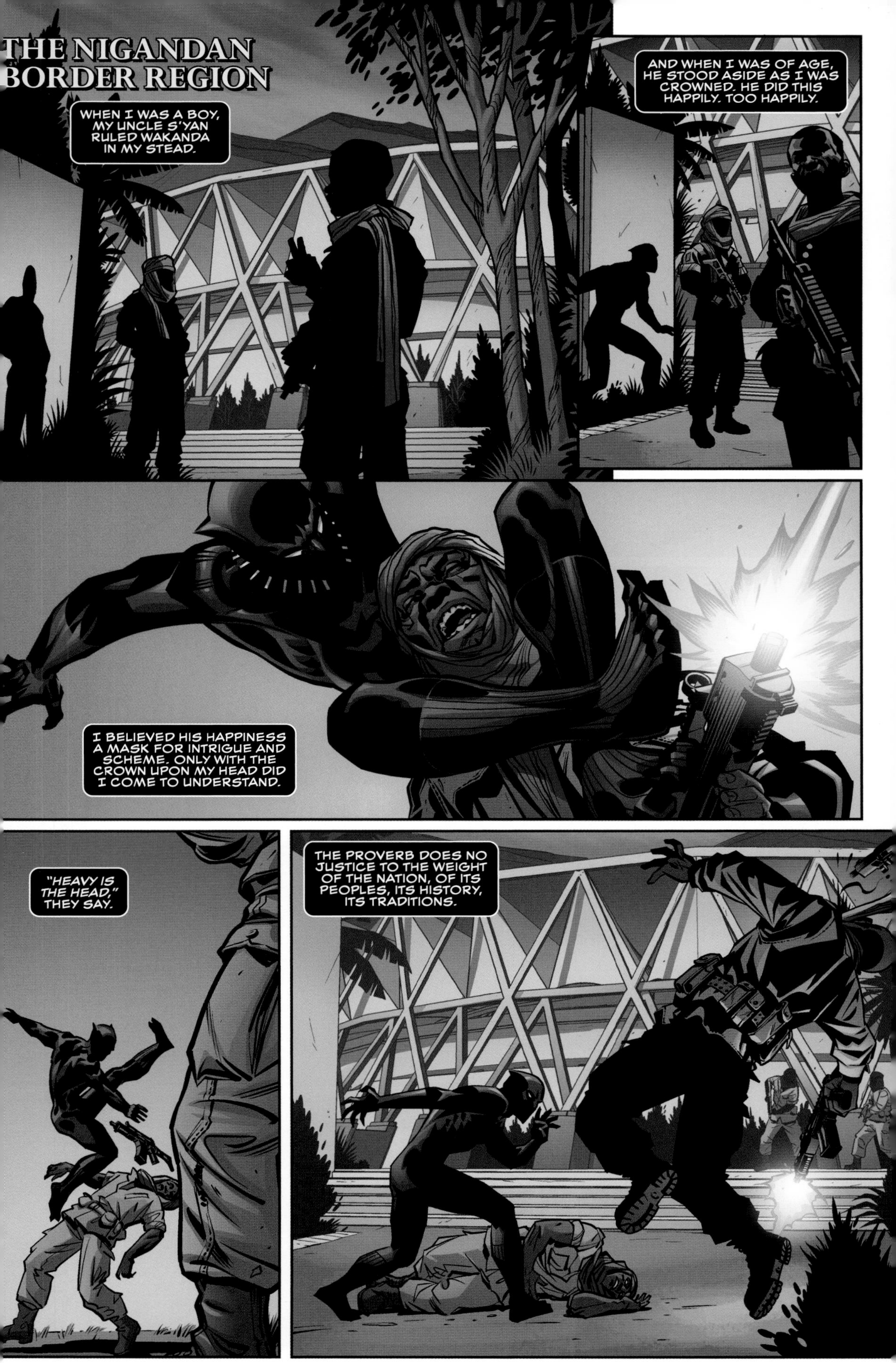
THE NIGANDAN BORDER REGION
WHEN I WAS A BOY, MY UNCLE S'YAN RULED WAKANDA IN MY STEAD.
AND WHEN I WAS OF AGE, HE STOOD ASIDE AS I WAS CROWNED. HE DID THIS HAPPILY. TOO HAPPILY.
I BELIEVED HIS HAPPINESS A MASK FOR INTRIGUE AND SCHEME. ONLY WITH THE CROWN UPON MY HEAD DID I COME TO UNDERSTAND.
"HEAVY IS THE HEAD," THEY SAY.
THE PROVERB DOES NO JUSTICE TO THE WEIGHT OF THE NATION, OF ITS PEOPLES, ITS HISTORY, ITS TRADITIONS.

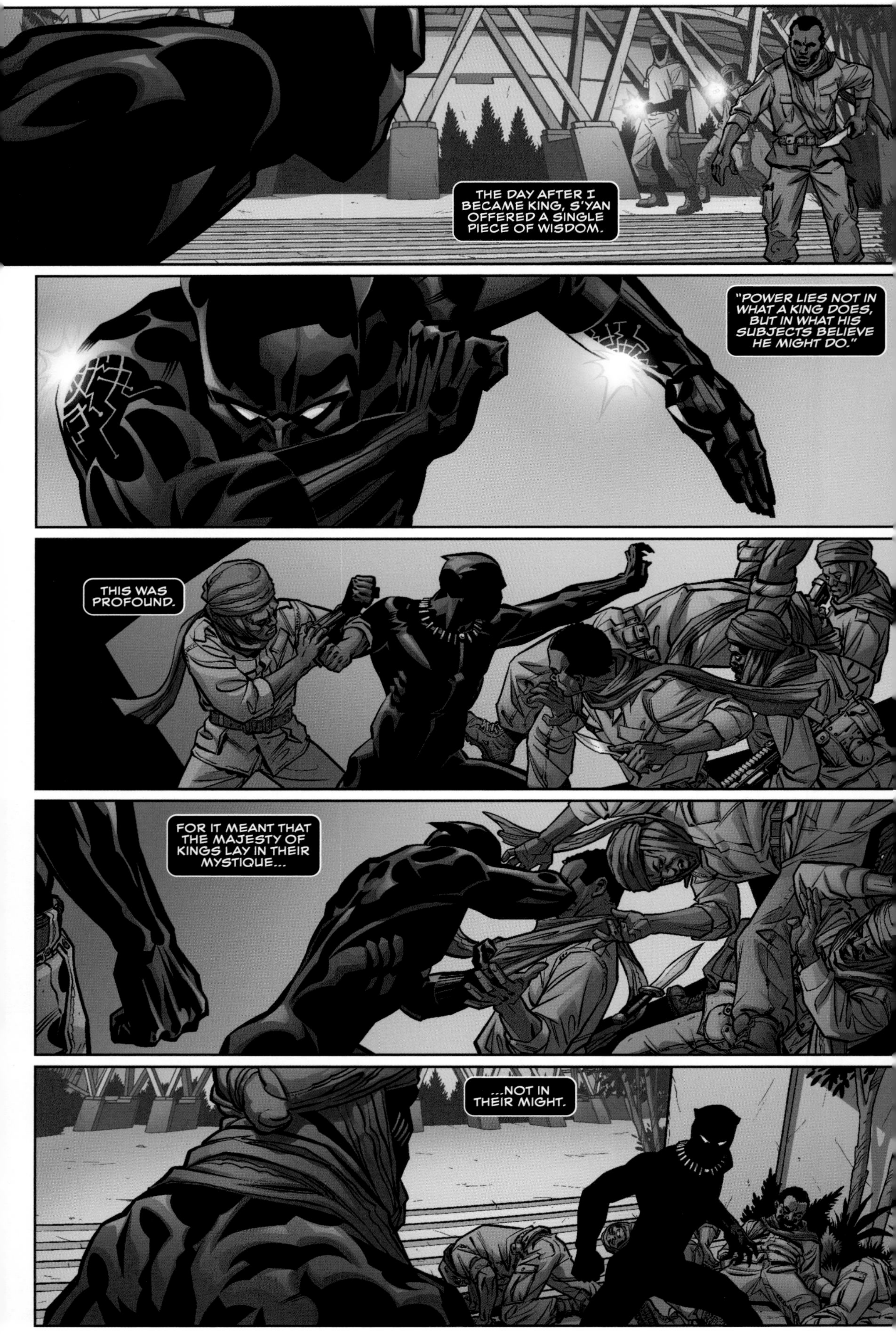
THE DAY AFTER I BECAME KING, S'YAN OFFERED A SINGLE PIECE OF WISDOM.
"POWER LIES NOT IN WHAT A KING DOES, BUT IN WHAT HIS SUBJECTS BELIEVE HE MIGHT DO."
THIS WAS PROFOUND.
FOR IT MEANT THAT THE MAJESTY OF KINGS LAY IN THEIR MYSTIQUE...
...NOT IN THEIR MIGHT.

EVERY ACT OF MIGHT DIMINISHED THE KING, FOR IT DIMINISHED HIS MYSTIQUE.

MIGHT EXPOSED THE KING'S POWERS AND THUS HIS LIMITS.

MIGHT MADE THE KING HUMAN.

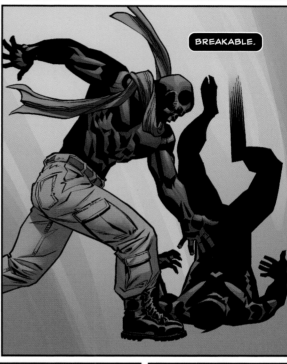

BREAKABLE.

AND SO SOME AMOUNT OF MY MIGHT I HAVE KEPT FROM THE WORLD...

...ALLOWING LEGEND AND MYTH TO FILL IN THE GAP.

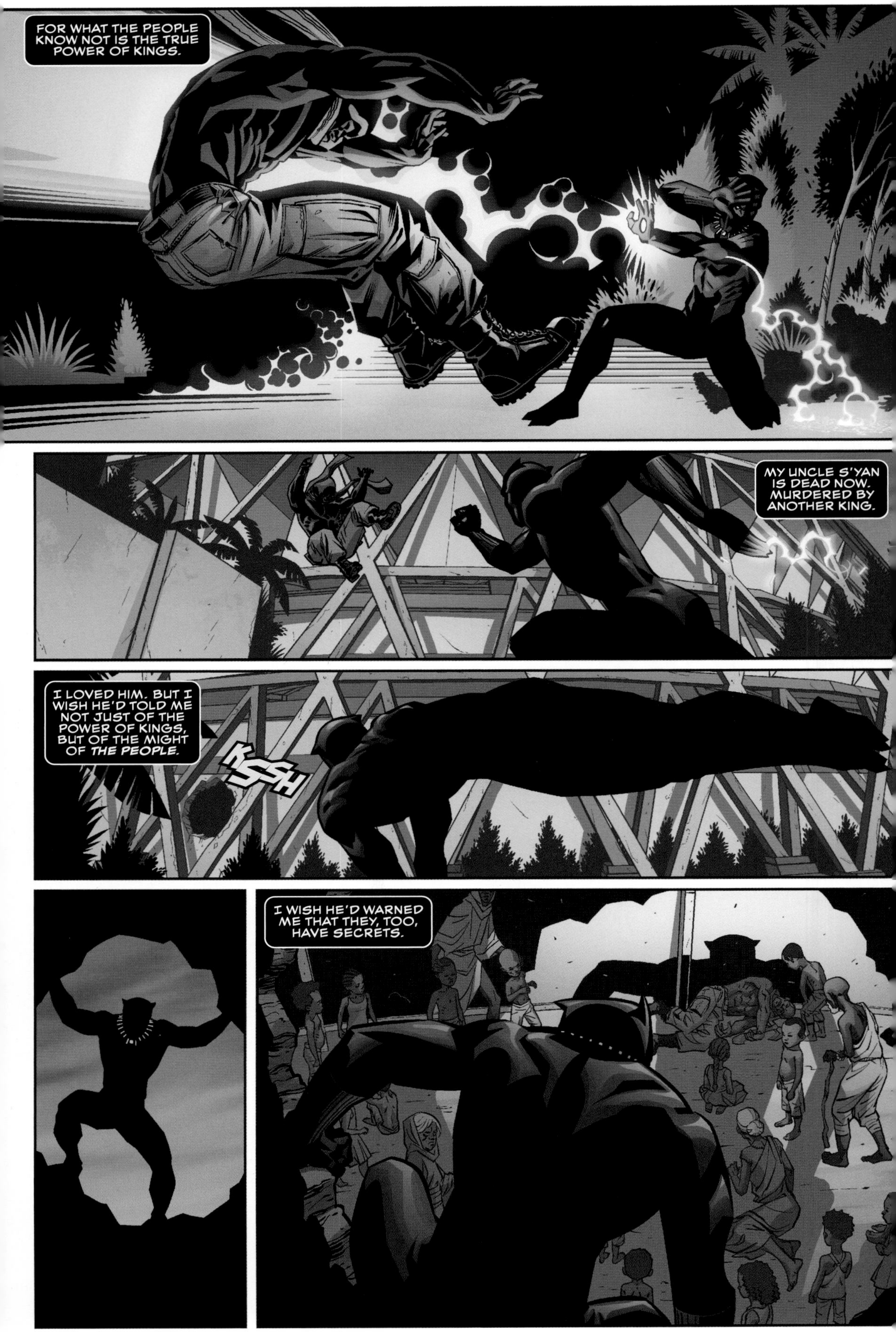
FOR WHAT THE PEOPLE KNOW NOT IS THE TRUE POWER OF KINGS.
MY UNCLE S'YAN IS DEAD NOW. MURDERED BY ANOTHER KING.
I LOVED HIM. BUT I WISH HE'D TOLD ME NOT JUST OF THE POWER OF KINGS, BUT OF THE MIGHT OF *THE PEOPLE*.
KSSH
I WISH HE'D WARNED ME THAT THEY, TOO, HAVE SECRETS.

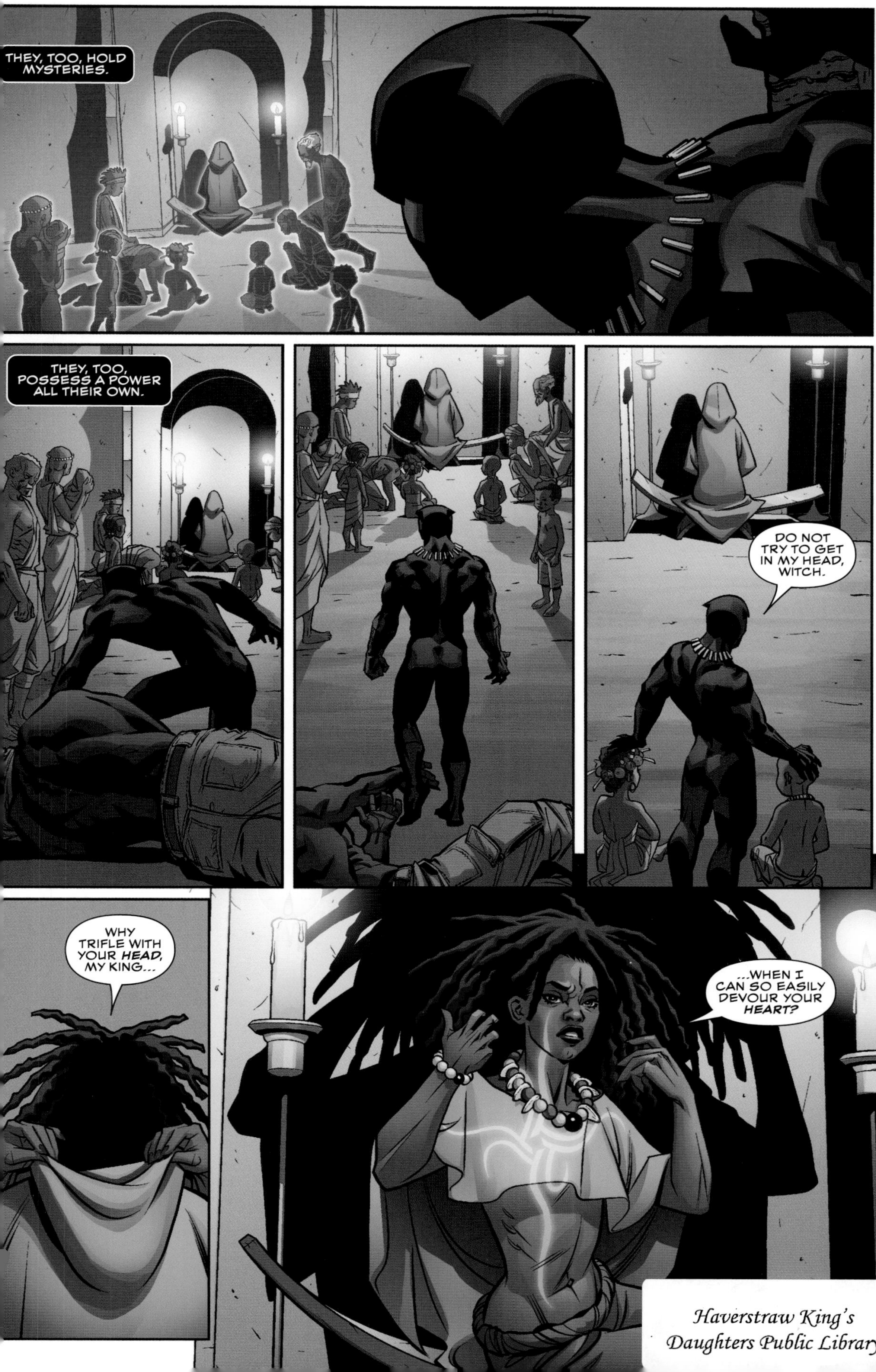
THEY, TOO, HOLD MYSTERIES.
THEY, TOO, POSSESS A POWER ALL THEIR OWN.
DO NOT TRY TO GET IN MY HEAD, WITCH.
WHY TRIFLE WITH YOUR *HEAD*, MY KING...
...WHEN I CAN SO EASILY DEVOUR YOUR *HEART?*

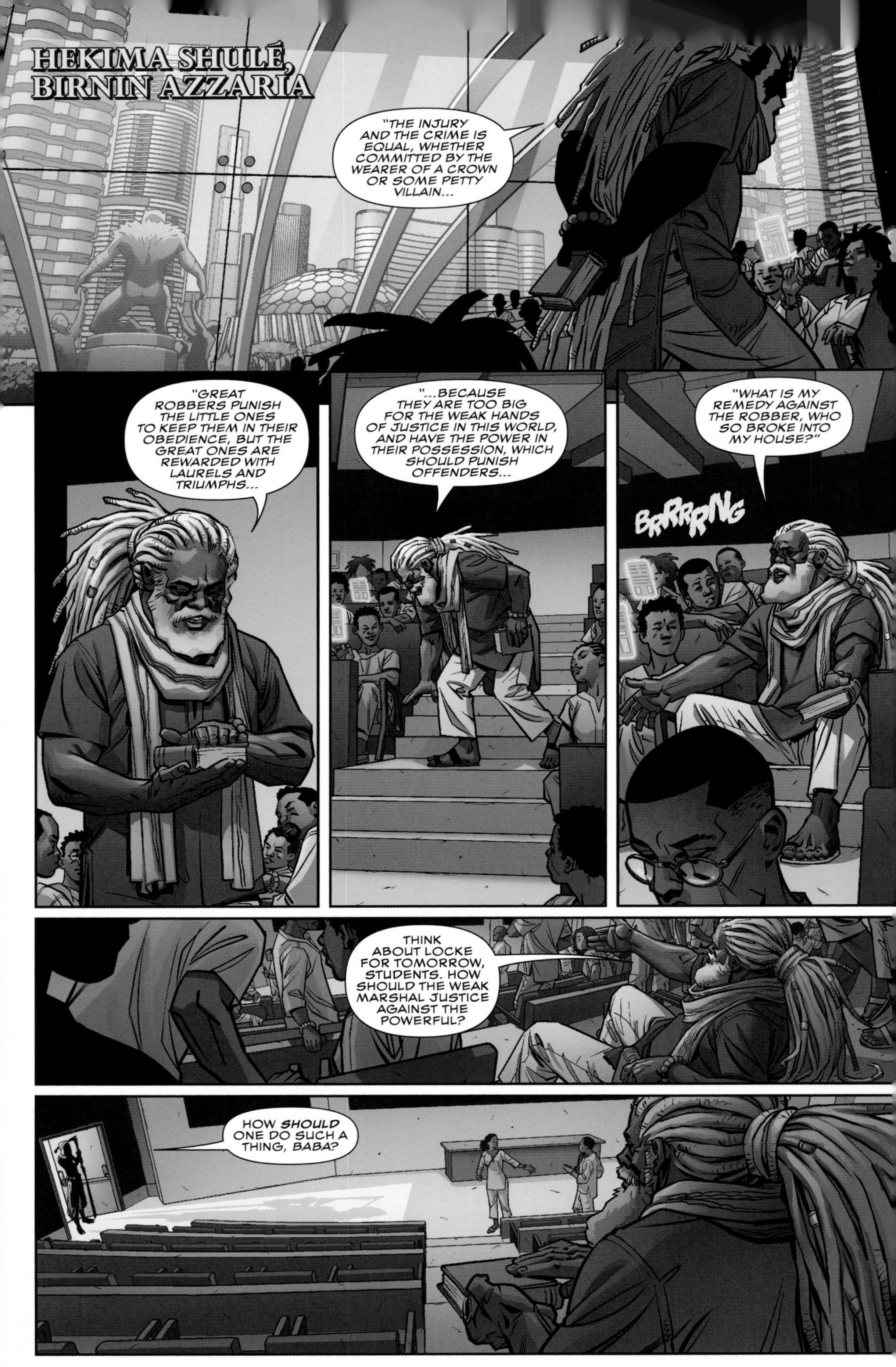
HEKIMA SHULÉ, BIRNIN AZZARIA
"THE INJURY AND THE CRIME IS EQUAL, WHETHER COMMITTED BY THE WEARER OF A CROWN OR SOME PETTY VILLAIN...
"GREAT ROBBERS PUNISH THE LITTLE ONES TO KEEP THEM IN THEIR OBEDIENCE, BUT THE GREAT ONES ARE REWARDED WITH LAURELS AND TRIUMPHS...
"...BECAUSE THEY ARE TOO BIG FOR THE WEAK HANDS OF JUSTICE IN THIS WORLD, AND HAVE THE POWER IN THEIR POSSESSION, WHICH SHOULD PUNISH OFFENDERS...
"WHAT IS MY REMEDY AGAINST THE ROBBER, WHO SO BROKE INTO MY HOUSE?"
BRRRRNG
THINK ABOUT LOCKE FOR TOMORROW, STUDENTS. HOW SHOULD THE WEAK MARSHAL JUSTICE AGAINST THE POWERFUL?
HOW *SHOULD* ONE DO SUCH A THING, BABA?

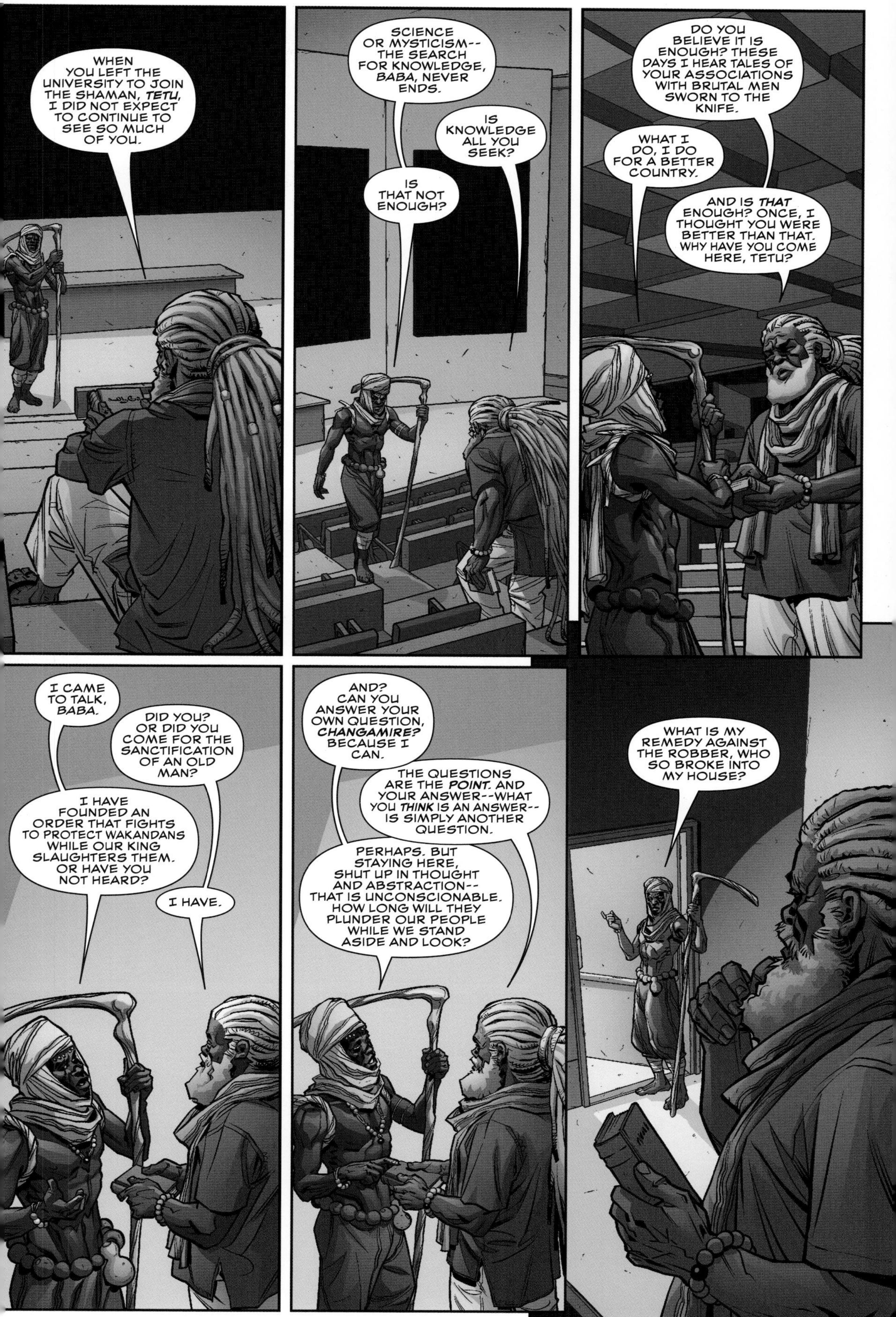
WHEN YOU LEFT THE UNIVERSITY TO JOIN THE SHAMAN, *TETU*, I DID NOT EXPECT TO CONTINUE TO SEE SO MUCH OF YOU.
SCIENCE OR MYSTICISM-- THE SEARCH FOR KNOWLEDGE, *BABA*, NEVER ENDS.
IS KNOWLEDGE ALL YOU SEEK?
IS THAT NOT ENOUGH?
DO YOU BELIEVE IT IS ENOUGH? THESE DAYS I HEAR TALES OF YOUR ASSOCIATIONS WITH BRUTAL MEN SWORN TO THE KNIFE.
WHAT I DO, I DO FOR A BETTER COUNTRY.
AND IS *THAT* ENOUGH? ONCE, I THOUGHT YOU WERE BETTER THAN THAT. WHY HAVE YOU COME HERE, TETU?
I CAME TO TALK, *BABA*.
DID YOU? OR DID YOU COME FOR THE SANCTIFICATION OF AN OLD MAN?
I HAVE FOUNDED AN ORDER THAT FIGHTS TO PROTECT WAKANDANS WHILE OUR KING SLAUGHTERS THEM. OR HAVE YOU NOT HEARD?
I HAVE.
AND? CAN YOU ANSWER YOUR OWN QUESTION, *CHANGAMIRE?* BECAUSE I CAN.
THE QUESTIONS ARE THE *POINT*. AND YOUR ANSWER--WHAT YOU *THINK* IS AN ANSWER-- IS SIMPLY ANOTHER QUESTION.
PERHAPS. BUT STAYING HERE, SHUT UP IN THOUGHT AND ABSTRACTION-- THAT IS UNCONSCIONABLE. HOW LONG WILL THEY PLUNDER OUR PEOPLE WHILE WE STAND ASIDE AND LOOK?
WHAT IS MY REMEDY AGAINST THE ROBBER, WHO SO BROKE INTO MY HOUSE?

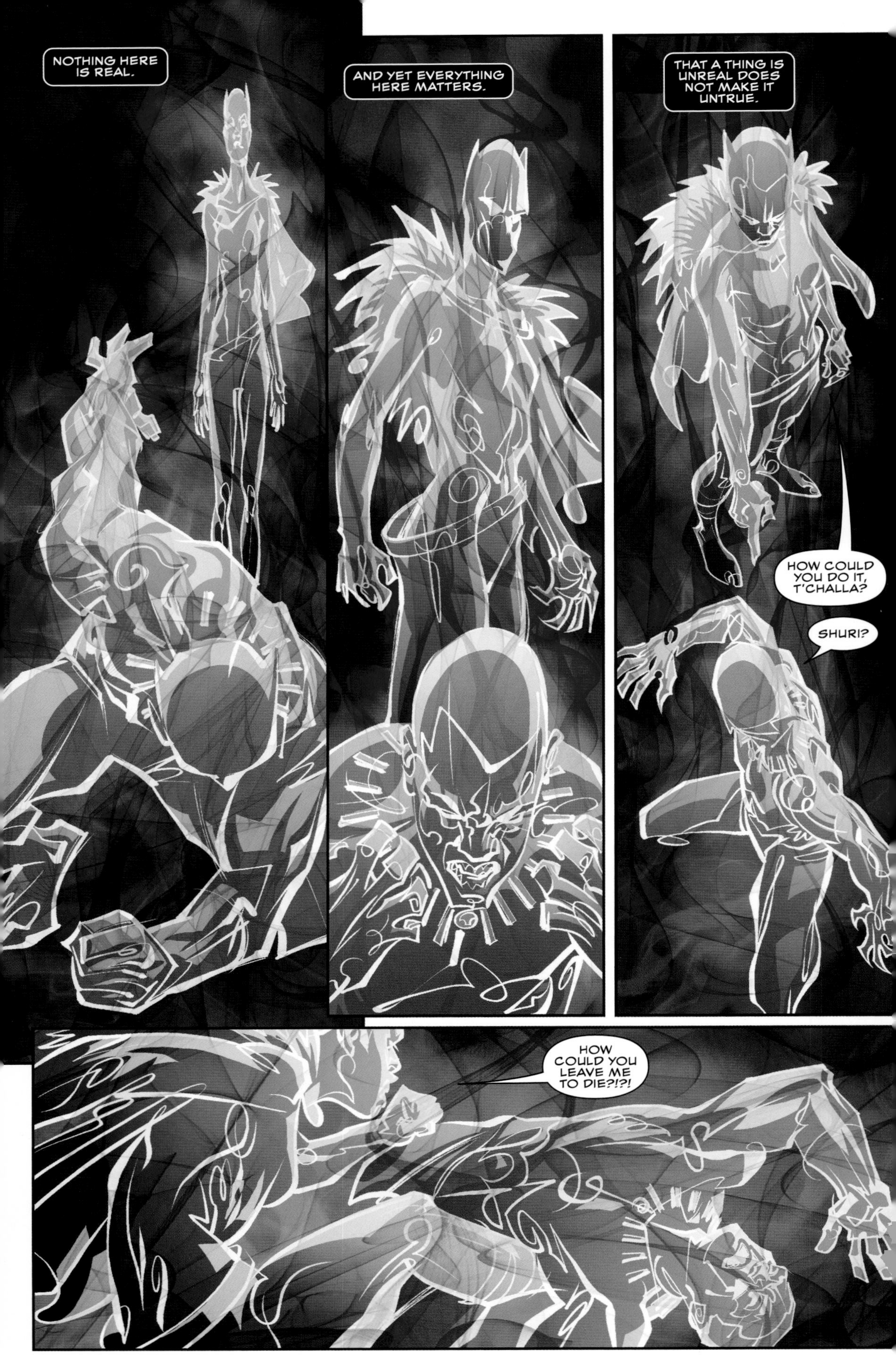
NOTHING HERE IS REAL.
AND YET EVERYTHING HERE MATTERS.
THAT A THING IS UNREAL DOES NOT MAKE IT UNTRUE.
HOW COULD YOU DO IT, T'CHALLA?
SHURI?
HOW COULD YOU LEAVE ME TO DIE?!?!

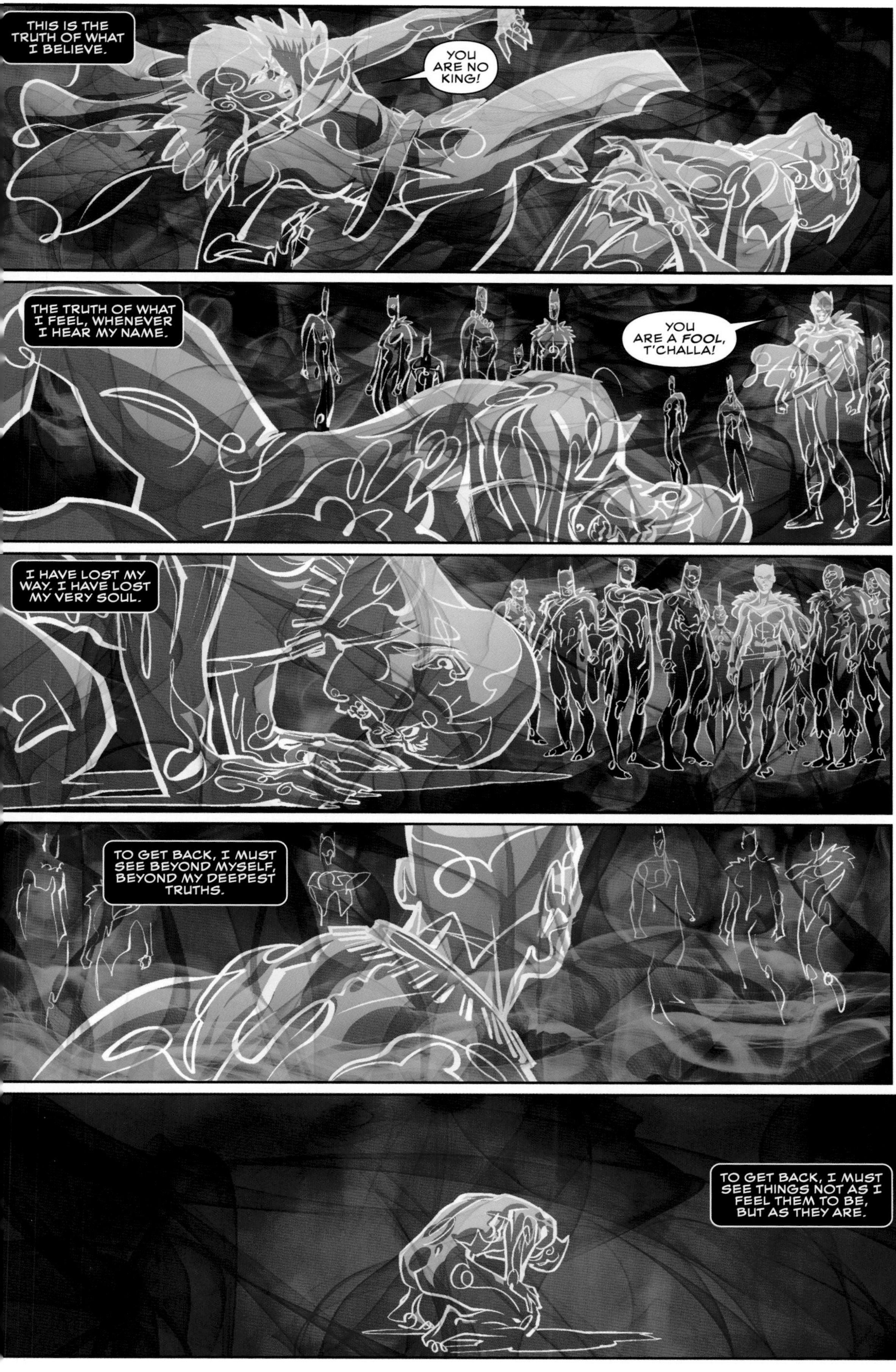
THIS IS THE TRUTH OF WHAT I BELIEVE.
YOU ARE NO KING!
THE TRUTH OF WHAT I FEEL, WHENEVER I HEAR MY NAME.
YOU ARE A *FOOL*, T'CHALLA!
I HAVE LOST MY WAY. I HAVE LOST MY VERY SOUL.
TO GET BACK, I MUST SEE BEYOND MYSELF, BEYOND MY DEEPEST TRUTHS.
TO GET BACK, I MUST SEE THINGS NOT AS I FEEL THEM TO BE, BUT AS THEY ARE.

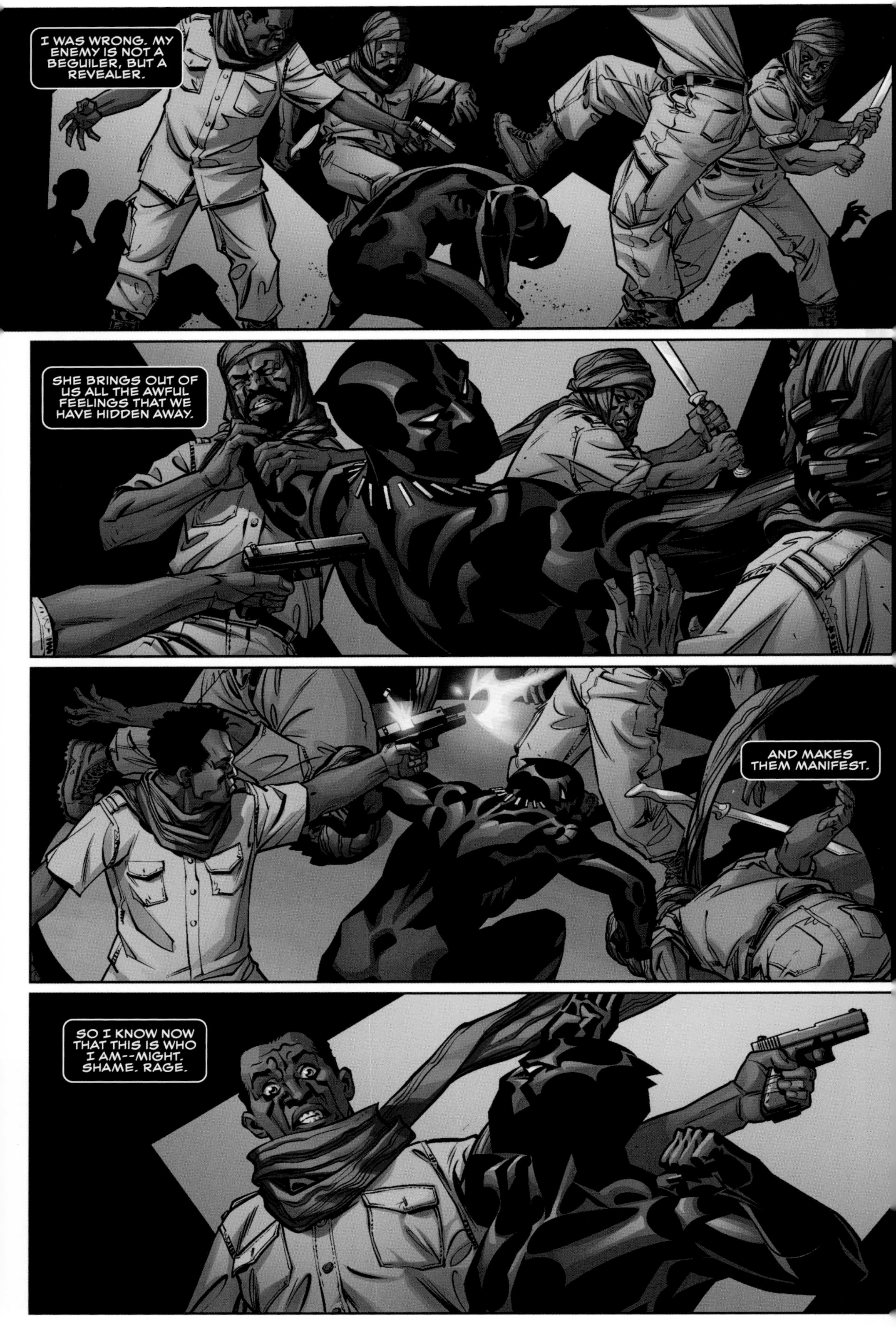
I WAS WRONG. MY ENEMY IS NOT A BEGUILER, BUT A REVEALER.
SHE BRINGS OUT OF US ALL THE AWFUL FEELINGS THAT WE HAVE HIDDEN AWAY.
AND MAKES THEM MANIFEST.
SO I KNOW NOW THAT THIS IS WHO I AM--MIGHT. SHAME. RAGE.

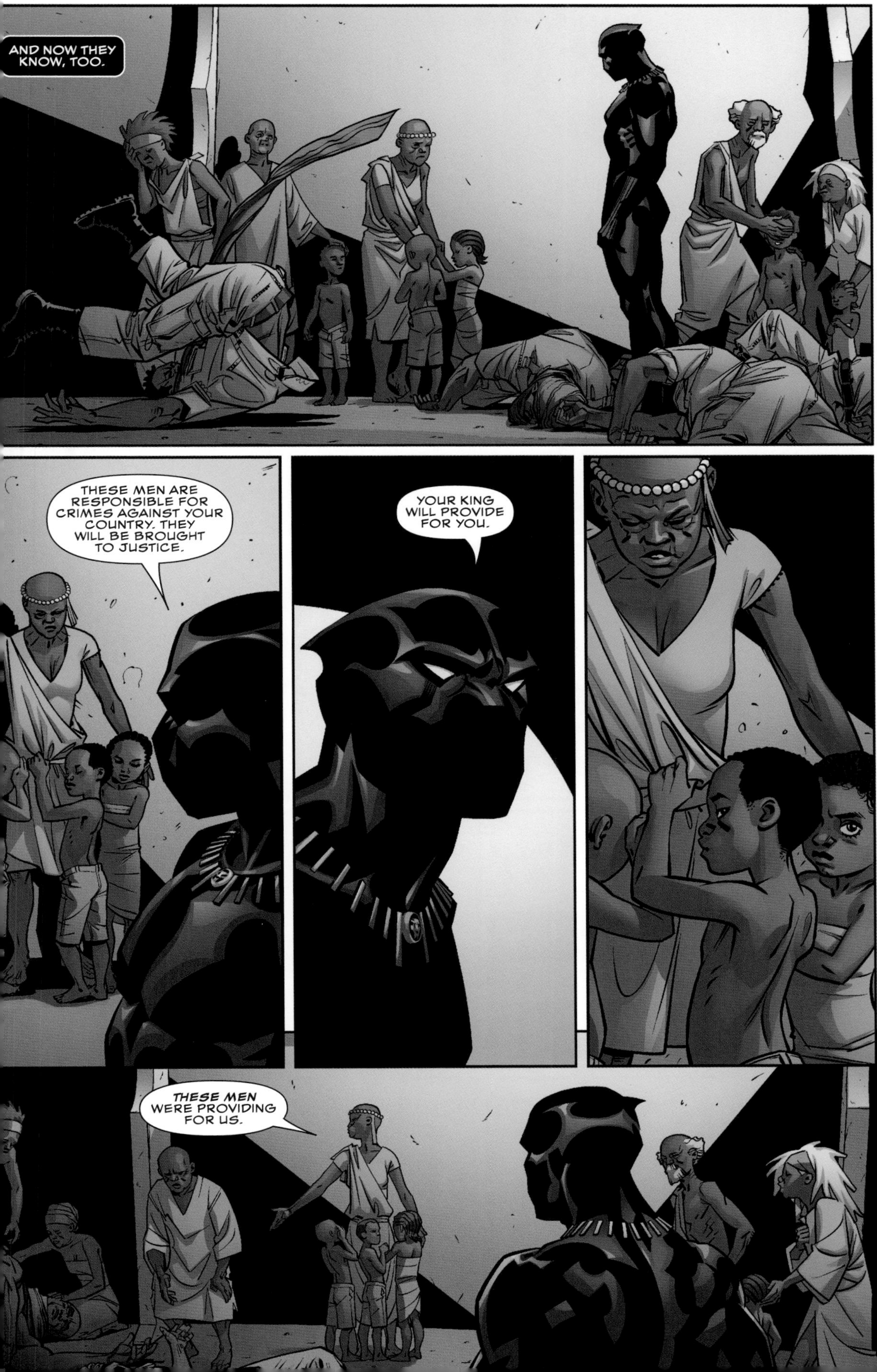
AND NOW THEY KNOW, TOO.
THESE MEN ARE RESPONSIBLE FOR CRIMES AGAINST YOUR COUNTRY. THEY WILL BE BROUGHT TO JUSTICE.
YOUR KING WILL PROVIDE FOR YOU.
THESE MEN WERE PROVIDING FOR US.

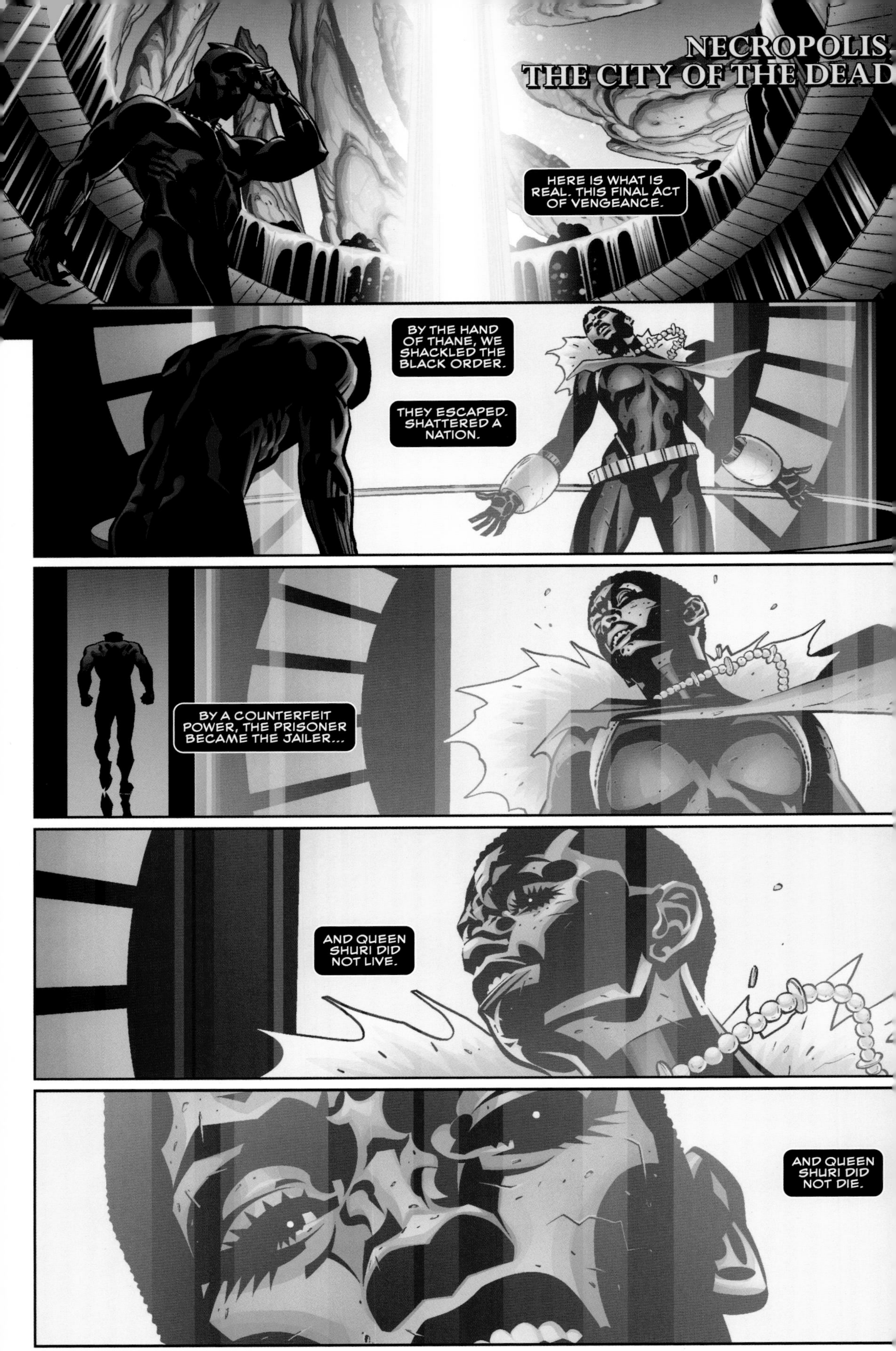
NECROPOLIS, THE CITY OF THE DEAD
HERE IS WHAT IS REAL. THIS FINAL ACT OF VENGEANCE.
BY THE HAND OF THANE, WE SHACKLED THE BLACK ORDER.
THEY ESCAPED. SHATTERED A NATION.
BY A COUNTERFEIT POWER, THE PRISONER BECAME THE JAILER...
AND QUEEN SHURI DID NOT LIVE.
AND QUEEN SHURI DID NOT DIE.

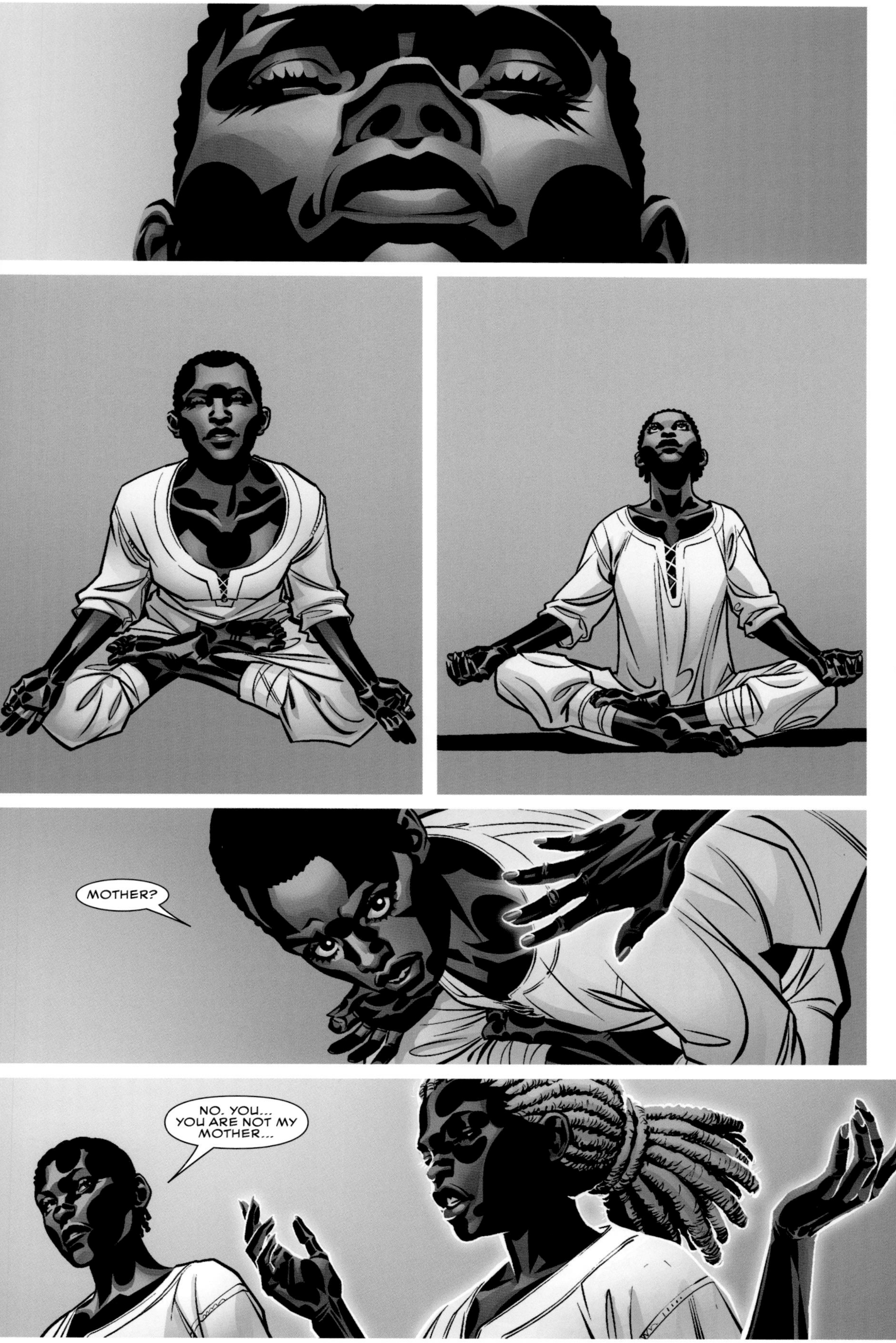
MOTHER?
NO. YOU... YOU ARE NOT MY MOTHER...

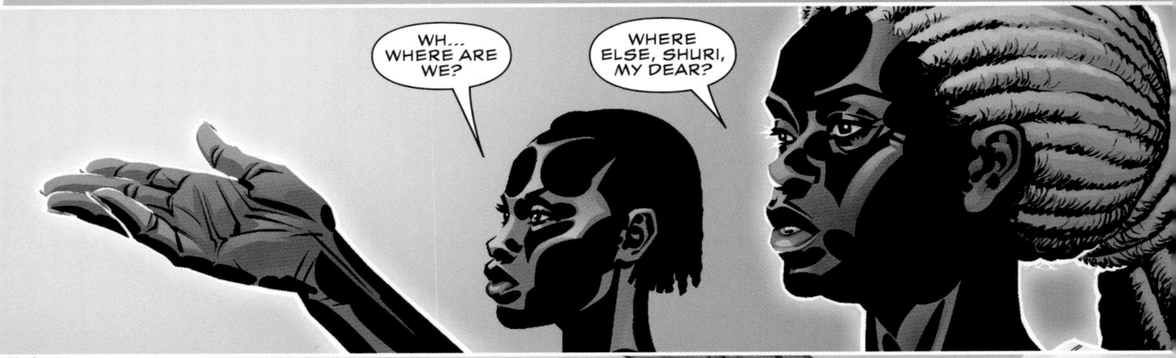
WH... WHERE ARE WE?
WHERE ELSE, SHURI, MY DEAR?

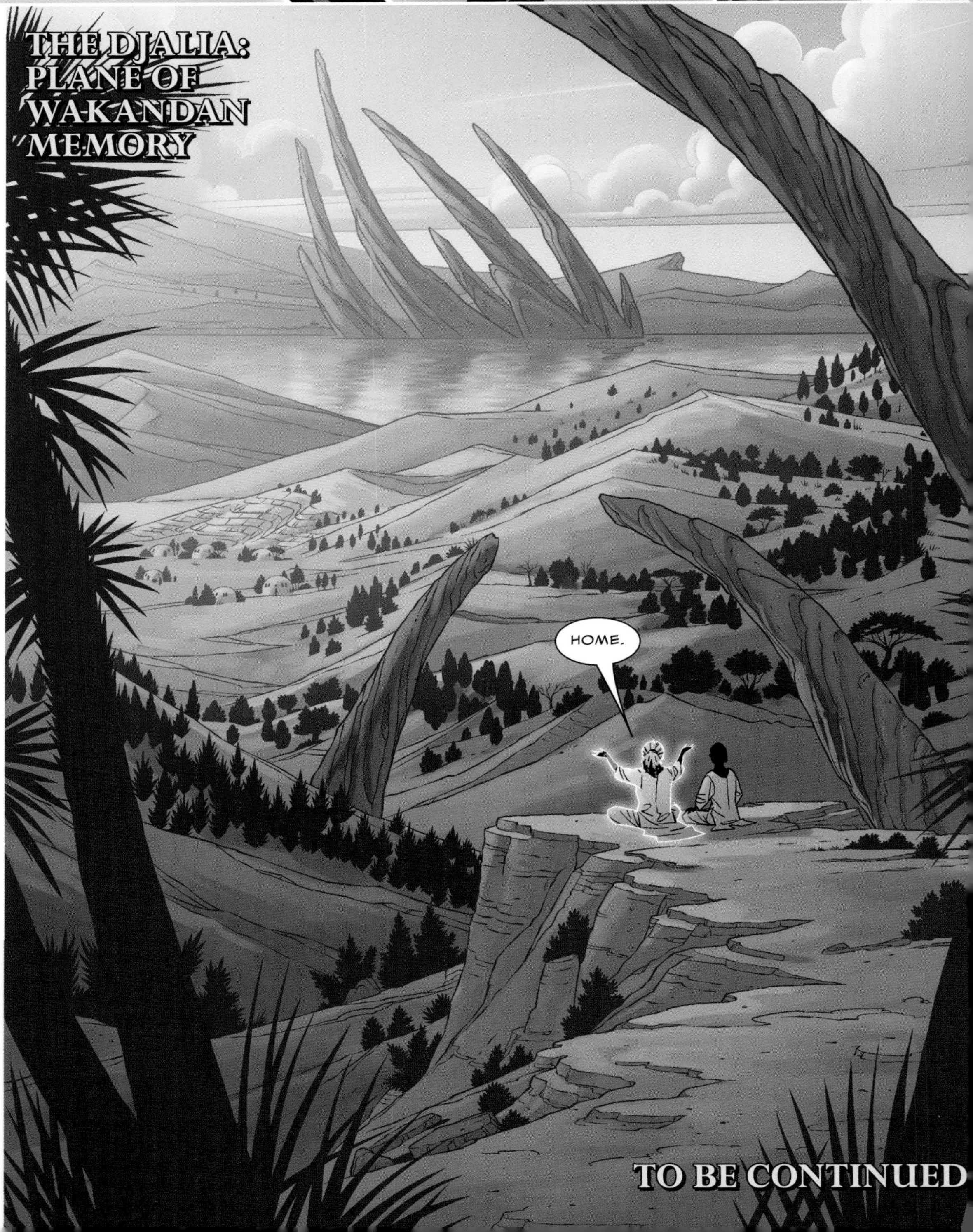
THE DJALIA: PLANE OF WAKANDAN MEMORY
HOME.
TO BE CONTINUED

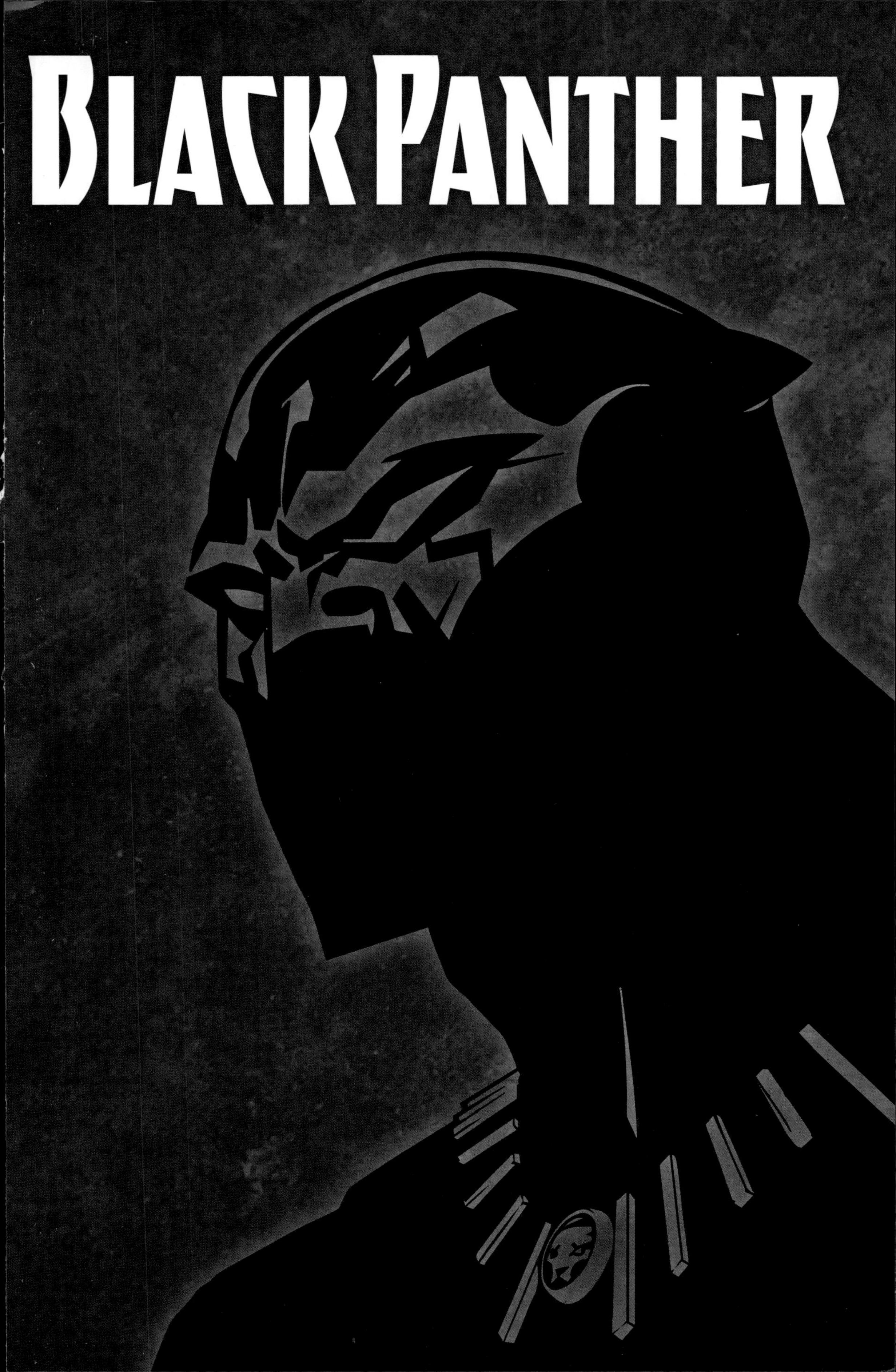
BLACK PANTHER

BLACK PANTHER

COLLECT THEM ALL!

Set of 6 Hardcover Books ISBN: 978-1-5321-4350-2

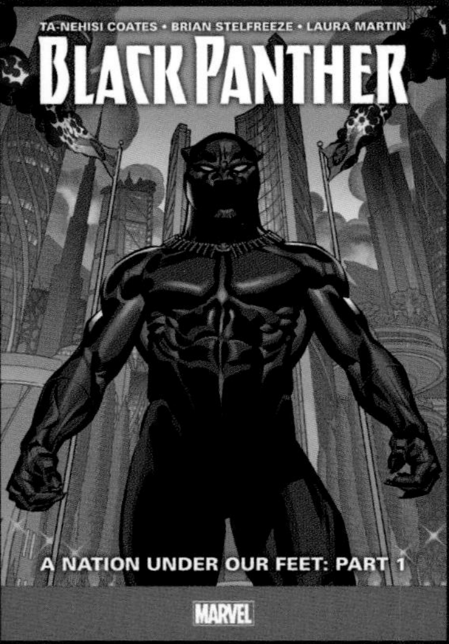
TA-NEHISI COATES • BRIAN STELFREEZE • LAURA MARTIN
BLACK PANTHER
A NATION UNDER OUR FEET: PART 1
MARVEL

Hardcover Book ISBN 978-1-5321-4351-9

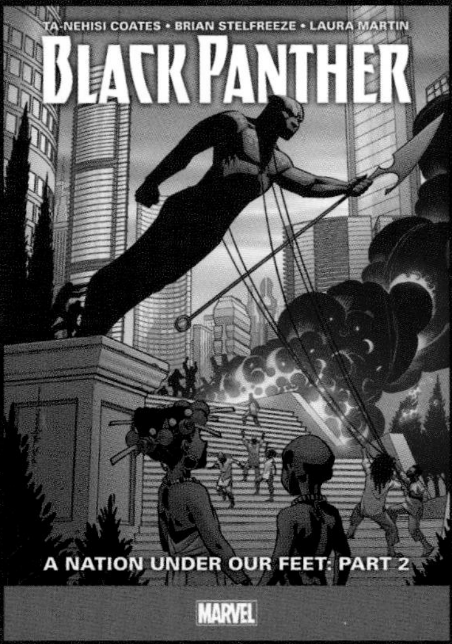
TA-NEHISI COATES • BRIAN STELFREEZE • LAURA MARTIN
BLACK PANTHER
A NATION UNDER OUR FEET: PART 2
MARVEL

Hardcover Book ISBN 978-1-5321-4352-6

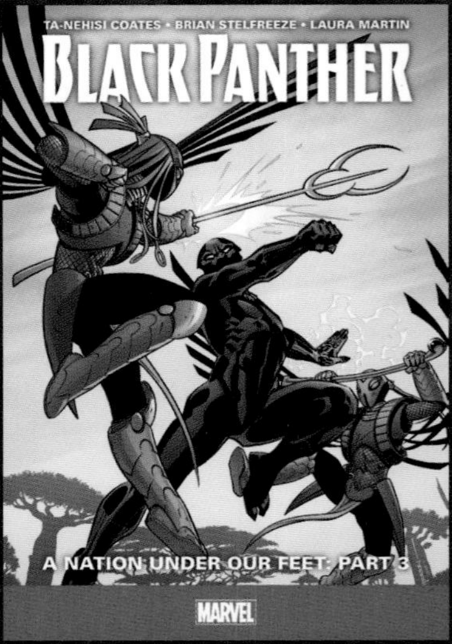
TA-NEHISI COATES • BRIAN STELFREEZE • LAURA MARTIN
BLACK PANTHER
A NATION UNDER OUR FEET: PART 3
MARVEL

Hardcover Book ISBN 978-1-5321-4353-3

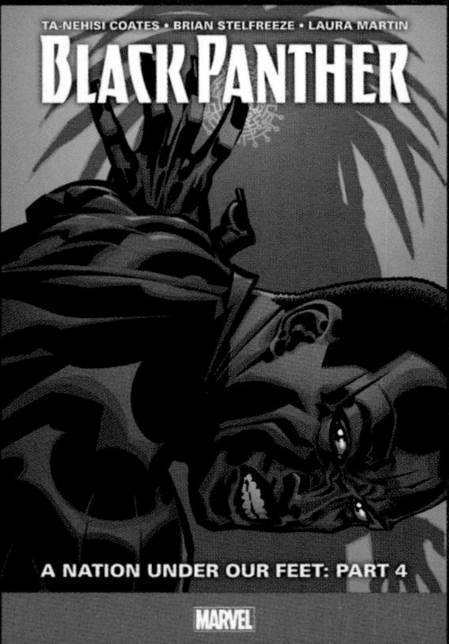
TA-NEHISI COATES • BRIAN STELFREEZE • LAURA MARTIN
BLACK PANTHER
A NATION UNDER OUR FEET: PART 4
MARVEL

Hardcover Book ISBN 978-1-5321-4354-0

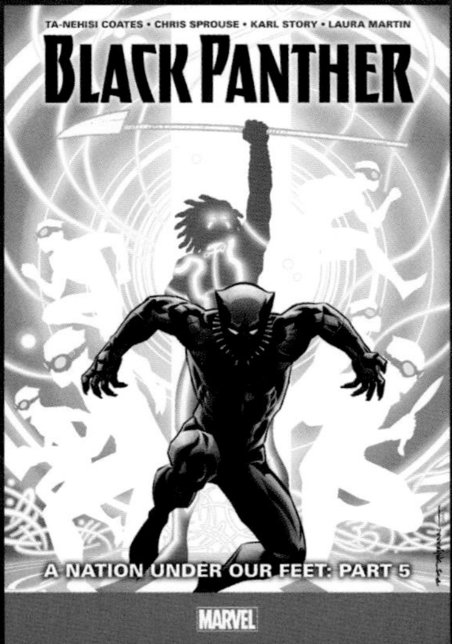
TA-NEHISI COATES • CHRIS SPROUSE • KARL STORY • LAURA MARTIN
BLACK PANTHER
A NATION UNDER OUR FEET: PART 5
MARVEL

Hardcover Book ISBN 978-1-5321-4355-7

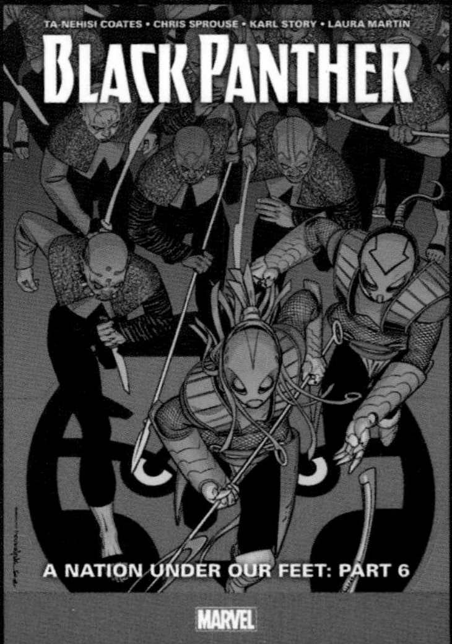
TA-NEHISI COATES • CHRIS SPROUSE • KARL STORY • LAURA MARTIN
BLACK PANTHER
A NATION UNDER OUR FEET: PART 6
MARVEL

Hardcover Book ISBN 978-1-5321-4356-4